Don't be greedy, Graham

A cautionary tale

Phil Roxbee Cox
Illustrated by Jan McCafferty

Edited by Jenny Tyler
Designed by Non Figg

Photographic manipulation by Nick Wakeford

First published in 2006 by Usborne Publishing Ltd., 83-85 Saffron Hill, London, EC1N 8RT, England www.usborne.com

This is Graham Preedy.

Graham Preedy is ever so greedy.

Graham always wants the first bite.

He always wants the last.

He wants the biggest portion,

and eats ALL his food so fast...

. . . and everyone's left sad and saying:

"Don't be greedy, Graham!"

At Jake's last birthday party,
Graham ate his birthday cake.

Yes, all of it!

"Don't be greedy, Graham!"

cried a very upset Jake.

Out shopping, Graham grabbed food
and drinks off each and every shelf.

He gulped and chewed
and slurped it down,
each mouthful for himself.

Once, Graham snatched a burger
from the person to his right.

Things turned very nasty.
There was scuffle and a fight.

He sneaked home
and said nothing.

He had a tummyache that night.

Next, Graham ate ALL the sandwiches after the school play.

The other kids went hungry
and chased Graham away...

"Don't be greedy,
Graham!"

called out a teacher (glad he didn't stay).

Graham is forever:

gulping. . .

chewing. . .

munching. . .

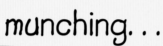

and chomping. . .

gnawing. . .

crunching. . .

14

. . . and everyone's left sad and saying:

"Don't be greedy, Graham!"

Come market day,
a herd of pigs is
led into the square.

16

Suddenly, they break free
from their owner, Farmer Dare.

17

Graham ignores the grunts and squeals
(as he starts off on his latest meal).

But Graham's teeth are so busy chomping,
he doesn't hear the pigs come romping.

He's swept up off his pudgy feet,
and carried down the muddy street.

The Preedy parents both give chase,
but soon lose sight of Graham's face.

(Uphill, the Preedys
are not so speedy.)

22

Poor old Graham, plump and greedy,
now which are the pigs and which is Preedy?

Now meal times no longer thrill.

They are just twice a day...

... and always swill.